Thank you to my Beta Readers

And, as always, to my First Reader,

Mel.

Contents

Vulgar Display of Power

The walls of Chemping were sturdy, built of stone, lined with arrow slits, and topped with parapets. Panicked soldiers scurried about the wall, and shouts and bells rang out through the city, mustering the rest of the fighting men.

Wisdom dictated that an army should strive to keep the sun at their back to hamper their enemies' vision. Sircius Everdeath and his army of metal men came upon the walls when the sun was high overhead and the wind was at his back. The lich stood proudly in front, a harsh contrast to the metal men of his army. He walked barefoot, his lordly robes caked in blood, with a sharp smile upon his face. Meanwhile, the army of one hundred metal men were shiny and impossibly clean, staring blankly back at the men like white-eyed locusts. Living suits of armor without the weakness or messiness of the flesh beneath.

There was something to be said for intimidation—the soldiers on the walls could clearly see the inhuman shapes and nefarious purpose of Everdeath and his metal men, the smell of oil and death wafting up with the breeze. It was a good start, but the old sorcerer could do better.

After all, the only thing he liked more than a good fight was a one-sided fight.

One of the men on the city wall, a captain or something, stepped to the front of the parapets, and mustered the steadiest voice he could. "Sircius Everdeath, we the people of Chemping order you to turn back, to stop your crusade of violence…"

"No. I don't think I will."

"Archers!"

Men began to scramble on the wall, and hundreds of bowstrings began to creak. Normally, such structures offered excellent protection against an invading army. The arrow slits especially; most were only four inches wide, and so the archer behind the slit was nearly invulnerable to incoming fire.

Sircius Everdeath did not have a bow, nor did his army; they didn't need them.

Everdeath held up a hand and magically seized one poor bastard. The soldier screamed behind the arrow slit, his agony briefly overshadowing the panic of the other soldiers. Then the lich pulled. What followed was a most inhuman squeal of metal and crunch of bone as the soldier was wrenched through a slit much too small for his body. The resulting mess flew across the field and landed at Everdeath's feet.

"Fire!" croaked the captain.

Hundreds of arrows soared from the wall. Clangs sounded from the field as arrowheads bounced off the metal men like rain off a tin roof. But most arrows, it seemed, came for the lich himself. He waved a hand and magic turned them away like an errant fly. Two pierced his right thigh, causing him a mixture of irritation and bemusement; he rather liked this outfit as stained as it was. He reached down with one knobby hand, broke off the shafts, and cast them aside. The arrowheads would fall out on their own.

The captain called for the second volley and the lich waved his hand again, ancient motions and sigils coming as easily to him as breathing. And with the motion, he said, "*Fulgur catenexus.*"

Flashes of light shone through the arrow slits as bolts of lightning arched from one soldier to the next. Though he couldn't see the carnage behind the stone, he could imagine it. The white hot bolts of electricity leapt from man to man in a blink, melting through armor, and pausing briefly to scour the organs before it leapt to the next closest living thing. Everdeath smiled.

Chain lightning was one of the lich's favorite spells, not just for its potency, but for its flavor. *Immolation* or *earth tremor* yielded similar deadly results, but both acted too suddenly, or covered the bodies afterward. So the lich could take little delight in their suffering. On the other hand, *Chain lightning* was just slow enough so that each subsequent victim saw death coming for them; they saw the man next to them fry and the man before that fall. And so Everdeath would walk the trail of bodies afterward, full of pride at the wide-eyed expressions of the victims.

But Sircius was getting ahead of himself.

Where hundreds of arrows flew before, two landed harmlessly at Everdeath's feet. As lightning finished tearing through the soldiers on the wall, bodies began thumping to the ground. The few survivors screamed and ran, abandoning their posts.

As much as the lich reveled in power and purpose, there was also something to be said for *fun*. Half a dozen cities Everdeath had razed to the ground, and each one was as gleeful as the last. Each one was a mix of playground, buffet, and theater.

The lich walked toward the towering double doors of Chemping. They were solid steel, each weighing as much as one hundred men. He could've manipulated the lynch gears, removed the barring, or even pushed aside the few poor bastards that still braced the door, but where was the fun in that?

Everdeath held up his arms and reached out with magic as if he were wedging his fingers between the middle seam. "*Apertun*," he commanded as he pulled.

The steel doors screeched and crumpled at the edges, then squealed as they were folded and torn back like paper. Bolts, hinges, and shards exploded into the air as the doors were ripped away and slammed to the ground.

As the gates fell, the screams of Chemping echoed over the field. Beyond the broken doors, the terrified denizens swarmed like ants fleeing a flood.

This day, Sircius strode through the gates first. With one hand, he waved away a group of soldiers, sending them hurtling across the remnants of a market. With the other hand, he grasped the incoming mace of another soldier, stopping it mid swing, ripped it from the man's hands, then bludgeoned him twice quickly with it, caving in both the breastplate and his helmet.

The lich turned his dastardly attention to a family fleeing into the side streets. "*Immolatalio*," he said, and with a flick of the wrist, the surrounding buildings erupted with flames.

To another escaping group, Everdeath conjured a wall of ice, then launched a hail of frozen spikes from his fingertips, pinning them in various stages of surprise and horror to the wall.

Ensnaring roots, pits of muddy sludge, streams of fire, acid rain, spontaneous combustion, suddenly collapsing buildings—the lich walked the streets with the flair of a conductor reveling in a masterpiece.

Then he sent his mechanical horde out. They swept through the streets like mad, murderous locusts, killing all those that their master didn't have time to chase down himself.

So long he'd spent cooped up in his lair preparing for such a campaign...

In his darkest moments, in those cold and indeterminate days in his lair, he'd wondered if it would be worth it; unfounded concerns now cast aside in the lich's glee.

And Sircius Everdeath would enjoy every moment, for one day it would end. One day there wouldn't be anymore cities left to raze or Terrans left to murder. One day it would all be ash—

That was the point, after all. It all had to end. The world of the humans, the world of the elves, everything in between, and all the gods who thought themselves above the fray.

END

To Walk in Dreams

Tylor's father used to say that you were everyone and everything in your dream. When Tylor dreamt and saw his bedroom or a castle, a girl, or a monster, he was not really seeing those things. He was seeing some part of himself.

His father said that dreams were the window to the mind. That they were the only way for a Terran to truly know themself.

This had been an especially troubling fact for the young boy to learn when his father appeared in so many of his dreams!

Tylor would always wake in his cot in the small room of his father's hovel—no matter whether he were dreaming or truly awake. He threw the covers off and stood up, then scrunched his toes on the scratchy, dusty planks of the floor. Then the boy would run through the house, without the thump of his steps or the creak of the boards. Silence was the key—If these things didn't make a sound, then Tylor knew he was dreaming.

Past the small hearth and out the front door to ghostly quiet streets. In the waking hours, the world was cobblestone streets and shacks, and every nook and cranny was filled with dark ash from the nearby factory. The children and people that were too old or haggard to work wandered the streets—their clothes speckled with ash and soot.

During the dreaming hours, the scene was much the same. Normally footsteps and the clack of cart wheels would mark the daytime, but not here, not now. And instead of his father working the long hours of the day in the factory, his father would be standing in the middle of the cobblestone street, waiting for Tylor.

His father's clothes, skin, and hair were dark from the soot of the factory. It had worked its way under his nails and into his wrinkles, but he smiled wide despite it.

That particular night and that particular dream, Tylor's father was picking up handfuls of ash and smearing them across the small houses opposite of theirs. Each broad sweep of his hand covered an impossibly wide swathe, as if the man were a giant; in three sweeps he painted a gray beach—erasing the rows of hovels and then the factory. After that, his father grabbed a handful of soot from his coat pocket and painted a vast black sea where the horizon had been.

"Come on, Tye. You try it," his father said.

So Tylor picked up a handful of ash from between the cobblestones and painted the hull of a boat. Planks of wood grew from the spaces between nothing, curving and joining together seamlessly. Two great, big sails were next, threads of night stretching and filling with dreams. It was as simple and easy as wishing it to happen.

It wouldn't be long now.

Tylor waded out into the muted water and climbed onto the boat. He pulled the rigging taut and felt the quiet wind fill the sail.

The boy was alone on the ship. His father was already gone, lost somewhere in those few water steps between dry land and the boat.

His father never stayed long—just like in the mornings before work at the factory, or in the evenings after. The old man woke long enough to eat, ruffle Tylor's hair, and walk out the door or lay down to sleep.

Tylor sailed out across the black sea until the ashen land disappeared. The gray sky turned to dusk and finally to dark, and Tylor was alone, stranded somewhere between a muted sea and a starless sky.

~

Tylor had made carriages of cold fire, castles of diamond bricks, puppies out of cobblestone and ash. He'd flown across the world on shooting stars, drank from clouds, uncovered a lost city beneath his house, and created automatons to work the factory.

Each night was a different adventure. Tylor's father waited for him out on the cobblestone street of his dreams. Each night, he showed Tylor some new sight or some new way of traveling across the dreamscape.

And Tylor had to remind himself that the man wasn't his father. They were not sharing the same dream. Tylor was merely creating a visage of him, the same way he created beaches and boats.

When young Tylor dreamed, he was talking to himself, interacting with, and teaching himself.

It was a strange idea, but the more Tylor thought about it, the more sense it made. He was asleep, and in his own little world. How could anyone else be there?

It was like playing pretend, except that in his dreams he could do anything.

~

One night, Tylor woke up in his dream, rose, and rubbed his toes on the floorboards. Then he ran through the hovel without making a sound.

Outside, the streets and houses were covered in crisp white snow—the kind that should've scrunched and crunched beneath his feet. The kind that should've sent him running back inside for shoes.

But that night, Tylor walked barefoot through the snow, silent as a ghost. He turned and admired the little footprints left in his wake. And when he'd run in a circle, Tylor stopped and scooped snow into perfect spheres, even bigger than he should've been able to hold. Thrice he did this, stacking them one atop the other to make a snowman. With some more swipes of his hands, he smoothed out the bottom into legs, slimmed its sides, and used the excess to make arms. Then the boy laughed at the skinny snowman with a fat, round head.

The moment and the laughter faded, and Tylor realized his father wasn't there. He wasn't waiting for Tylor anywhere along the cobblestone street. He was always there.

"Dad!" Tylor called, but no one answered. No one else from town was wandering the snowy streets. The world was painfully quiet and still. Tylor was alone.

The whole world was silent as a dream.

As Tylor looked frantically from one end of the street to another, someone appeared in the middle of the road. For a moment, he thought it might've been his father, but excitement quickly drained from the young boy's face and dread swelled in his throat.

The man wore a long white robe, the hood of which completely covered and draped in front of his head, while the ends draped across the ground—blending in and disappearing amidst the snow.

But its sudden appearance hadn't startled Tylor, nor did its hunched pose.

It was the robe that made the boy recoil. It had not the texture of fur or snow, but skin. Pale white, thick with folds and belying thin green veins. Its arms hung slack at its sides, sheathed in the cloth, and barely distinguishable from the body of it.

The boy had seen nightmares, even conjured them and banished them. But as Tylor stared at the hideous figure before him, he knew that whatever it was; it wasn't from his own mind.

It was a stranger in his dream.

"Who… Who are you?" the boy asked.

The thing didn't respond.

In a fit of fear, Tylor grabbed a handful of snow and swept his hand across the street—desperately trying to paint over the creature.

But as the houses and the street turned shades of ash gray, *the thing* remained—the same dreadful icy white.

Tylor reached down and grabbed handfuls of stone and flung them upward, the handfuls of stone turning to mounds of earth in the air. In moments, the boy had covered the town in a great mound of earth, a mountain of a hill.

But *the thing* merely stood on the slope, unperturbed.

So Tylor leapt into the sky, long golden wings spreading from his back. Upward he climbed. Above the city, above the distant mountains.

He looked back, afraid to speak, afraid to breathe.

The thing was growing. It stood as tall as the clouds. Nearly tall enough to look Tylor in the eye as he flew.

No matter how high he flew, there was no end to his pursuer. When Tylor burst through the clouds and looked down on a sea of white fluff, *the thing* burst through, its head and shoulders towering like a colossus over the world.

Soon, Tylor had flown so high that there was nothing but clouds beneath him—somehow he knew that the mountains and even the ground itself was gone. The boy flew and flew, desperately trying to find a new world to flee to—any world to flee to.

Soon the golden wings he'd made grew tired and weak. He panted for breath, and each flap began to pain him.

And when the boy fell toward the clouds and his golden wings disappeared in a puff of feathers, Tylor opened his mouth to scream—no sound came out. And he was no longer moving. Tylor was floating above the clouds as easily as he could stand on the ground.

He turned and found the towering *thing* diminishing until it looked him in the eye. Its hooded face was still hundreds of feet tall and wide, and its body lost beneath the clouds, but Tylor no longer felt the same dread as he looked upon the pale folds of its cloak.

"You like to dream," the creature said to him, its voice breathy like a whisper born upon the wind.

Tylor nodded, his throat dry and breath still.

"Come with me."

"...I can't. I have to go home. I have to wake up and see my dad."

"Dreams, Tylor… They are wondrous, aren't they? We can live for years in our dreams, while we sleep for only one night. You do like to dream, don't you?"

The boy nodded, for the *thing* spoke the truth about dreams and time, and about Tylor.

"Come with me," *it* said, "and I will give you the power to walk through as many dreams as you want."

Tylor's eyes opened wide in excitement, but he quickly looked downward, past the clouds, toward some imaginary spot where his father was waiting.

"But what about my dad?"

"You will live a hundred lifetimes before your father wakes."

The boy couldn't argue with the creature. His head spun with wonder at the thought of dreaming *more*. Tylor didn't much like being awake. If it weren't for his father, the young boy would spend all day sleeping and dreaming—trying to escape. Here was *someone* trying to help him do just that.

Besides, Tylor was still dreaming, and so he could have many more adventures before his dad started to miss him.

It took all of a few seconds for Tylor to agree to go with the creature.

"Then speak the words, little one. Search your mind and you will find them."

At first, Tylor wasn't sure what it was talking about, but then strange words came to him as if he'd dreamed them.

"*Accipe me tecum*," the boy whispered.

As he said the words, the creature reached up with white, titanic sleeves and pulled back its hood.

As the hood fell away, darkness filled the sky, as if an ocean of ink had been spilled. Blackness and dots of light poured over the clouds and blotted out everything, including the creature.

The little white dots grew and grew until each was somehow both as numerous as stars and as big as a wagon wheel.

In each pocket of light, Tylor saw a world—a dream: He saw vast oceans full of shining fish and strange slithering creatures. Castles that rose into the sky, twisting and turning until it looked like they had to topple over. Endless fields with ironwood trees planted by giants. Chariot races across the sky that left fiery trails in their wake.

He could've spent a lifetime deciding which world to visit first.

But eventually, Tylor picked a snowy village filled with elves and faeries. As he slipped through into another world, he knew that it was someone else's dream—

And that the *thing* was right behind him.

END

The Lightning Nymph

Len Baatly was a mage at the Institute of Charlemagne. His specialty was metallurgy—the intersection of smithery and magic. It was well known that fire could change the properties of metal, burn away the impurities. Quenching a hot blade in water did similarly. Heat and cold, fire and water.

His latest and most poignant experiment came the day he watched the institute's lightning rod explode during a storm. That's how it started: He merely wanted to see if lightning could be used to forge steel as fire could. After examining the old rods, he confirmed that electricity changed the metal's composition—though it was such an intense and short-lived energy that it was nowhere near the changes found in a smelted blade. Len decided he needed to run proper experiments. That's what took him to the top of Ghoten Mountain.

The Eastern side was prone to storms for most of the year, so Len set up shelter near the summit and then built a tower a short hike away. It was a shoddy thing, little more than a hollow frame made out of magic-locked bricks, but it suited his needs. Len was a mage, not an architect. He'd scarcely gotten the tower up before the first storms came that spring. That first night he could merely watch as lightning struck the tower repeatedly, great arcs coming down like an anvil of the gods and splitting the sky. Even from his camp, it sounded as if the mountain might crack.

The next day, he spooled wire from the tower to his workshop and through several lengths of steel. His first experiment was ready, and when the next storm came, he watched as lightning traveled from the tower and to his camp, just as he planned.

But he needed more.

So he climbed the tower, ready to affix the testing steel to its summit, but the next storm came suddenly, sweeping over the land like a torrent. He barely made it down before the lightning started. And when he was nearly back to camp, the world went white and silent.

For a moment, Len Baatly thought he was dead. There was nothing but white. No sound. He couldn't even feel his body. But from the ether came the soft crackle of electricity. White gave way to waves of blue, and a Terran outline.

It was *her* that was blue, Len decided. The lady shimmered in his vision like she were made of lightning. Her smile pulsed with life.

Len was hypnotized.

A moment later, she vanished, taking the light and the soft hum of electricity with her.

Cloudy darkness filled his vision, and Len realized that he was on his back on the rocks. He hadn't made it back to camp. HIs clothes were ragged and smoldering, his skin a mix of red and pink. His ears rang. His shoes were gone, his toes black.

He tried to stand, but struggled, as if his body was ten times heavier than it had been before. He finally rolled over, gasping bile onto the rocks when the rain came. It fell softly on him, and had soaked him through by the time he got to his feet. He limped back to camp and thanked Movernus that it was a short stumble, then sent for help.

The storm was already gone by the time his assistant arrived and helped him back to town. All the while, Len Baatly thought of the lady of lightning.

~

It took Len a month to recover after the mage's accident on top of the mountain. Jagged scars covered his right leg, and wrapped around his stomach and left arm. He couldn't decide if it was a boon or a cruel twist to have such a pattern imprinted on him. But Len didn't dwell on the souvenir—the thought was as fleeting as lightning.

During his recovery, he asked his apprentice to carry on with his experiments. Each evening, Len Baatly would insist on hearing the results of the day's experiments, and whether any strange apparitions had been seen—each night he drifted off to sleep, disappointed.

When he was well enough, Len strode up the mountain with his cane—all thought of his research was gone. He thought only of *her*. He raised an even larger tower, gathered even greater coils of wire. Dragging the blocks up the mountain and building the tower strained his magical power, but he wouldn't be denied. For the briefest moment, he considered standing atop the tower when the storm came—he would be struck and he would see her again, but surely he would perish.

Instead, Len Baatly constructed a circular table of wire and bolts and steel. The next time the storm came, lightning struck the tower and shook the rocks beneath his feet. Blue power surged through the coils and coursed to the table. The contraption glowed a bright blue, and for a moment—just a moment—Len Baatly saw her.

Lightning wound through the coils and jumped across the center—highlighting the form of the blue goddess. She shimmered like sunlight on water. She curtsied and then began to dance—nothing like Len had ever seen. Her body became formless and abstract, like pure and pulsing energy, disappearing and reappearing as lightning jumped through the table.

For a few perilous breaths, Len stared, and then she was gone. He wept that night—tears and rain falling on the mountain as one.

~

Len Baatly became obsessed with the lady in the storm—the Lightning Nymph, as he'd come to call her. His apprentice and all his fellows at the Institute of Charlemagne knew it—Len Baatly knew it. It was not his first obsession, but those who knew him feared it would be his last.

Two months after the accident on the mountain and the doctor informed Len that he would need a cane the rest of his life. He limped up to the mountain and started on his next experiment. The table that had held the Lightning Nymph for those few moments had been destroyed, and Len had been forced to try other methods. All had failed so far. So he returned to the table—to his original design.

He constructed a cage of wire mesh big enough for him to stand in, and fixed it to the tower. Then he bound the cage in wire coiling and pylons. So thick was it that he had to climb under through a jagged, narrow passage in the rocks. He waited for a storm, then climbed inside, leaving his cane behind.

Clouds rolled overhead and then came the rolling thunder and the smell of ozone.

A deep fear overtook Len Baatly—an urge to run, to flee—but he was frozen, unable to move.

The world went white and then faded to blue.

"You came," said the lady. "I was beginning to think you'd forgotten about me."

Rather than a boiling outline of electricity, her form was blue, soft, and supple. Before the spellbound mage could reply, the Lightning Nymph curtsied and began to dance. She whirled around the cage, somewhere between electricity and shimmering water.

Len Baatly was spellbound, in love with the most beautiful thing he had ever seen. Even when her form appeared inside the cage and danced around him, Len couldn't move. He could only stand still as the hair on his arms and his head began to lift, as his skin prickled.

The world grew blinding and white, and Len Baatly knew peace for the last time.

END

Hanging Lanterns

Julene tended the garden, hanging lanterns every night. There were sixteen of the heavy silver things, and each was lined with runes she could not read. There was a ritual to their placement: While Julene hung them one at a time on the holly trees, the master of the house chanted in his father's tongue. Julene didn't know what he said each night, and the master would not say, but she knew that each lantern had its own words. Julene told herself they were prayers, but the old man wouldn't confide in her.

For ten years, Julene tended the garden, hanging lanterns every night. Sixteen beautiful silver things, each unique, and each in its own place. Every evening while she did this, her master watched from the manor. In ten years, he'd never told her the reason for the ritual, nor the meaning of his chants, so Julene created her own stories. The first lantern was wrapped with koi fish, and as she lit it, color bled through the fins where the metal was delicate and thin. Julene told herself they were the first fish to swim in the seas after Movernus made the world. The second lantern depicted a mountain range littered with spindly trees as old as the dirt they clung to. She imagined the first god dwelling somewhere beneath the stone, slumbering beside the rockmen.

The third lantern was for great beasts of tooth and claw, but the pressings in the metal were all hard lines and little fur, as if they were leaping out to get her. Julene could hardly tell what creatures they were supposed to be as she looked over the faded silver. Fourth was for birds and winged things: Bats, harpies, angels, greccion, and things for which Julene had no name. For all the things that took to the sky and flew away from the vicious things of the lantern before. The fifth lantern was for the forest where so many of those creatures dwelled, and for the old fey gods of antler and bone, their twisting forms indistinguishable from the fallen branch and bramble. Somewhere in the metal are two tiny druids, those humans that settled the Odhran forest, and some say still linger there.

Julene hung the sixth lantern. It was for the elves, the first and oldest Terrans, walled off in the city of Novissimé and fighting a holy war. The elves that fled spoke little of these things, but all humans know the fables. Seventh was for magic and sorcery, those ancient rites and scrawlings. A web of geometry covered the silver, and occasional bright gleams of blue bled from the runes. Sometimes, when Julene hung the seventh lantern, she felt pangs of recognition—she knew she could not read the arcane scrawlings. The feeling was more akin to trepidation at standing beside a cliff's edge. She had never fallen from such a height, never known the pain, yet her body trembled, all the same.

The eighth lantern was for the first humans, the ones that harnessed fire, tools, and first tasted of magic and meat, before there were words for any such things. If the lantern of magic made her tremble, the eighth lantern did the opposite. It filled her with hope and wonder she hadn't known since she was a girl. The ninth lantern was for vampyres and wicked things that followed the dreams of humans. Though humans crawled out of the forests and raised towns and cities, those hunters followed. The ninth lantern depicted a city, and in the alleys, men fell prey to hunters that looked the same as they.

Julene hung the tenth lantern. It was for ships and freedom and exploration. Treacherous waters shimmered in the silver— the passage of Digsonee Strait. Of all the places on the continents of Eadruin and Ozequn and the Frozen Isles, it alone was feared beside beast and wicked things alike. Julene was about to hang the eleventh lantern when she looked to the great house and found that the master wasn't there—wasn't watching her. She stopped, left the rest of the lanterns on the ground beneath the holly trees, and ran to the manor.

The servants brought the master of the house to his bed. Julene brought him a bowl of water and doused his head with the damp cloth. The nurse attended to him—he didn't have much time left. The old master looked to Julene and told her that he could finally go now that she was tending to the lanterns. Julene didn't understand, for she'd been doing the same task for these ten long years. The master shooed her back to the garden to finish her nightly task.

Julene walked solemnly back to the garden. Tears fell as she hung the eleventh lantern. Again, she saw the delicate wings of angels and thistle bushes. It was for goodness and mercy, and Julene prayed for these things for the master of the house— surely he would have mercy.

Julene hung the twelfth lantern in the holly trees, crisscrossed by roads and smiling faces. It was for families and trade. Though she did this dutifully, her thoughts were still troubled by her master's suffering. By the time she hung the thirteenth lantern, no tears fell from her cheeks. This one was for poetry, art, and beauty. It would be all the more beautiful if she didn't know what the next lantern depicted. The fourteenth was for heroes and myths. Great warriors and mages battled across its face, their strikes so powerful they blurred across the face of it.

The fifteenth lantern made Julene shudder. It depicted suffering and sorcery. Emblazoned on the front was the vile sorcery Sircius Everdeath. Flames surrounded him and the world burned, but not even he lasted forever. The sixteenth lantern was filled with swirling shapes, even more beautiful than the patterns of the koi fish. Julene didn't know what the lantern represented, though she thought it meant *uncertainty*.

What comes after the end, she wondered.

The next morning, the master of the house passed. Julene was called in by an officiate of the estate. She was a kind woman, dressed in black, and she read aloud three sentences—the only part of the old man's will that pertained to her. They handed Julene a lantern—the seventeenth such lantern—a week's pay and granted Julene her freedom. Julene left the estate that evening, looking only once at the untended holly trees, and clutching her own lantern. It was completely smooth and blank, and the note inside told her to one day stamp her own artwork on the lantern. Its light flickered across the old stones, lighting a new path for her. As she descended her steps swelled with confidence.

END

Guardians of the Forest

Rain pelted the shutters of the small hut, and thunder sounded in the distance. The boy Cheseldine drew the covers up to his nose.

His mother had turned to go, but the boy called after her. "Tell me a story, mama. Please."

She turned and sighed. He hoped dreadfully that she wouldn't tell him he was too old for such things. His father already thought that.

His mother walked over and sat on the edge of the bed. She cradled the table candle in her lap and it cast playful shadows about her face.

"Alright," she said, "But just one."

"One you haven't told me before?" Cheseldine asked, his words muffled by the blanket.

She thought for a moment, then decided on one.

"Long ago, when humans were young, and elves already old, great owl-kind lived in the forests." They were giant owls of incredible colors, but that kept themselves cloaked and invisible as they prowled the forest. "They were the guardians of

the wild, the grove, and the thicket. They were called Resnocti—"

"How did you meet them?"

"Who said anything about meeting them?"

Cheseldine sank a little lower in his bed and looked at the
candle.

"I did meet them," his mother whispered.

The boy turned back to his mother, eyes wide.

She said, "Now, are you going to let me tell the story?"

Cheseldine nodded.

"As I was saying, they were the guardians of wild things and
forest things. They were enormous creatures, as tall as the tav-
ern in town, with wings that could stretch across the street.
They flew silently through the trees, and their feathers could
turn the colors of leaves and bark so that they were invisible
while they roamed the forest."

"But how did you find them?"

"I'm getting to that part." She took a breath. "When I was
about your age, I wandered into the forest. Mind you, it was a
foolish thing, but I did it. I got lost, and as the sun started going
down, I got very scared. All manner of creatures live in the
forest, including those that like to eat little children."

"Mama…"

"It's okay. I was all alone, and it was nearly dark, when I
heard a growl coming from the brush behind me. I saw narrow
eyes and pointed teeth. It was a jaguar!"

Again, the blanket was pulled up to the boy's mouth as he
listened with trepidation.

"I was so scared that I couldn't even run. The jaguar crept
closer and closer to me. I could see its fur glistening in the
moonlight. Just when I thought it was about to pounce, I felt
a rush of wind, like a storm had blown through the forest. I

fell to the ground, and when I looked up, something was holding the jaguar so tight that it couldn't move.

"I heard a horrid screech, and saw the head of an owl appear above me. Its feathers were sleek and brown, its beak was open. As it screeched, the feathers grew brown, like wax dripping down a candle.

"Then it hurled the jaguar into the woods. I didn't see where because I couldn't take my eyes off of the giant owl. I watched as the color faded from it, leaving green leaves and thin branches in its wake—disappearing right before my eyes.

"I called out to it, told it not to go. I said I was lost and that I needed help.

But the owl said nothing—not until I asked its name. It's name was Chesen, a Resnocti, and like me, he was alone.

"Why are you all alone?' I asked."

"At that, Chesen laughed. It was a deep rolling laughter like thunder, and each laugh brought more brown color to the feathers of his head and neck. Chesen had been alone for as long as he could remember, since even before humans had built cities or worked fields. Back when we lived in the forest and didn't venture out into the open.

"Back then there were a hundred Resnocti, each as big and as silent and fierce as Chesen. Some had feathers that were stone gray, others that were brilliant blue or fiery red, but each was invisible as they flew through the forests. It was only when they spoke that they allowed themselves to be seen."

The boy spoke up. "What happened? What happened, mama?"

His mother grew quiet. "Some say that a monster just as powerful as the Resnocti scared them away, but that's not what I think. I think instead, the owls ventured out from their home, and that they each found their own forest to rule over. Just like one day, you'll grow up and open up your own tannery and have kids of your own."

"But what happened to you that night in the forest?"

"Chesen guided me home. He walked beside me through the forest. He told me all about his brothers and sisters, and about the dangers of the forest: Kuatari and Sendiv, the elders with feathers the color of cracked stone, and the youngling Waundy, with feathers as fine as new grass. There was Janis— the fey goddess of all the jaguar, and the forest gods Arietes and Aryvon…

"As Chesen told me all of this, his feathers would come alive with color, but he had to talk slowly because if he talked too much, his whole body would be colored and he would lose all his magic."

The boy's eyes were wide as he listened to his mother, and finally he said, "Chesen… Like Cheseldine?"

His mother smiled, "Yes, my sweet. You're named after a guardian of the forest."

"Did you ever see him again?"

"A few times, but never for long. Once, he saved me from a bristleback." She waited while Cheseldine pulled the covers over his face, then peeked at her fearfully. "I stumbled across it as I was hurrying home. It was huge and gray, with great big tusks that stuck up past its eyes. It stamped the ground, and right before it was about to charge, Chesen flew down from the trees, grabbed the bristleback, and hurled it into the forest. It ran away, squealing.

"Another time, I got caught in a downpour. The rain was coming down in huge, fat drops. Chesen found me and walked me home for the third time. He held his wing over me, shielding me from the rain."

"Can I meet Chesen, too?"

His mother pursed her lips like she was unsure of what to say. Finally, she smiled. "Not tonight, and not tomorrow, but one day. Until then, don't go wandering through the forest like I did."

She reached out and made to tickle his stomach to emphasize this point. Cheseldine tucked himself into a ball and nearly rolled over.

He asked, "Is that because Chesen isn't here anymore?"

As soon as Cheseldine asked the question, he regretted it. His mother's face scrunched again.

"The Resnocti aren't there anymore, sweety. That means Chesen, too. Besides, he passed along some of his knowledge of the forest to me, just as I'm passing it along to you. And rule number one is don't go into the forest."

"Okay. Okay."

"Promise?"

"Yes, mama."

"Good." His mother kissed Cheseldine's forehead and left him to sleep.

As she left, Cheseldine thought of her when she was young and wandering the forest, and the stories that she told him of his namesake. As the rain lulled him to sleep, the boy tried to think of those happy things and not of the horrors that lurked in the dark corners of the forest—

Tried not to think of those things that swallowed gods as if they were children.

END

The Hedge Maze of Greensnow Manor

Greensnow estate overlooked the Gelid Sea—the southernmost stretch of the Frozen Isles. Chunks of ice crowded the water even in the summer months. The manor sat on the edge of the cliffs, three hundred feet above the churning water. Snow, be it heavy or fine powder, covered the mossy ground in nearly every season.

Every other month, the *Little Sparrow* brought provisions and mail to their island. Once yearly, family from the North visited, or perhaps friends of the family would summer there.

No one stayed for the winter, save for the Greensnows and the families that worked the grounds.

It was a beautiful and desolate place, and to Natalia Greensnow it was home.

~

Natalia was a young girl of ten when mother let her wander the grounds by herself. She had sense enough not to trouble the workers too long with her questions, nor to stray too close to the cliffs, and not to enter her father's study while he's working, or not working—not to enter her father's study at all, really.

Even back then, most days Natalia occupied herself. She would wander the grounds, stopping by the kitchen to see what Bernice was preparing for supper that day. Sometimes, the cook would explain how to make a dish, and little Natalia would listen and try to commit it to memory. It seemed a silly thing, since Bernice would always be around to cook for them, but the cook seemed to enjoy talking to her and Natalia enjoyed listening.

The youngest Greensnow was no longer permitted to play with Bernice's son, Isiah, but she was still allowed to visit. Isiah spent more of his time tending the grounds with his father. Natalia would find them hauling coal for the furnace, mending this or that broken thing. Isiah would smile warmly, and his father would tip his hat.

In her walk around the grounds, Natalia would inevitably pass by the hedge maze—the only other place she wasn't permitted to go. The maze was as old as the estate itself, dating back some six generations of the Greensnow family. Supposedly, it was to remind the original Greensnows of their original home on Eadruin, where the weather was more temperate. Father told her the hedges were bolstered with magic to survive the harsh winters, and that it was never to be entered—ever. She knew the hedges were ten feet high, but to young Natalia, they might as well have been towering green cliffs. The entrance might as well have been a yawning and ominous portal.

Every time she passed, Natalia would look upon the entrance and the walls of the maze with a mix of curiosity, wonder, and dread—the three emotions welling in her like icy waves.

In the spring, Isiah and his father would go inside to trim the hedges, carrying shears and a ladder. Natalia would watch them disappear inside and listen for the telltale sounds of the shears or the ladder. Anything to assure her that they were still in there and hadn't been swallowed up by the hedges.

Spring after spring they did that, Natalia always listening with bated breath—even as she grew older, she couldn't shake that formative apprehension of the hedge maze.

Next, she'd walk to the stables and along the horse pastures. They were workhorses, giants even from a distance. Usually, only Vitta or Saran would come over and stretch their necks over the fence to be pet. Sometimes, Bernice would give her carrots to bring to the horses. On those days, all eight of the great beasts would trot over and vie for her attention.

When she was done walking the grounds, she would retire to the manor's library. Aside from the great hall, the library was the largest room of the house. The shelves stretched up two stories tall, all the walls lined with brilliant spines, like a rainbow emerging from glass.

In the afternoons, Natalia would slink into the library, peruse the shelves (carrying a small stepladder with her to reach the higher books). Her process for selecting a book was quite random—some days the girl chose books based on their spine or an intriguing title. Other days she'd flip to the back and read the snippet about the author, waiting for one that piqued her interest. Other days, something on the grounds might catch her imagination and she would seek a non-fiction book about it (these were confined to the second floor). Once it was whaling, geography another, plants of the known world, and cultures of the Frozen Isles.

Natalia would select a book and retreat to one of the towering windows and curl up beneath several blankets. She would read until the sun went down. On the rare occasion that a book bored her, she would close it, gather up her blankets, and trudged back to the shelves with the mound of warmth wrapped around her. On the occasion when she couldn't climb the ladder with her blanket pulled taut, she'd drop her blankets and put the book back as quickly as possible. It was for this reason, that even if a book bored her, Natalia usually suffered through it, choosing warmth and boredom instead of cold and the chance at something more interesting.

Perhaps it was because of her quiet existence on the cliffs of the Frozen Isles that Natalia rarely got bored with the books she chose—that she could find something of interest in almost every volume she plucked from the shelf. She would read until the sunlight faded and she was forced to retrieve an Everlit candle to read by.

Natalia adored the routine of it all. Even during the rare days that the Greensnows entertained visitors and traveled to the other islands, Natalia longed for the comfort of the familiar.

~

Occasionally, Natalia's father or mother would be in the library taking a break from their correspondences or bookkeeping. Father would be sitting at one of the small tables, usually using the time to read an adventure novel and smoke his pipe, filling the room with herbs and fruit. He would greet his daughter by name, and then continue with his reading, barely pausing to look up at her. Natalia tried not to take this personally, for her father was a busy man and like that with everyone he interacted with.

Mother would perch beside the window and beneath a blanket of her own. She would close what she was reading, and watch as Natalia chose a book, then run over to the window. Then the pair would slump against one another and disappear into their own worlds.

Her mother was fond of romances and sweeping histories. Sometimes she would turn to her daughter and point to a paragraph, asking Natalia to read it. Most times, it was a simile or a metaphor that she wanted to share. Mother was fond of beautiful descriptions—of ones that fit together like imperfect puzzle pieces. Descriptions that were so different they changed the way young Natalia thought of the world—

A blanket of night. History and art that lay within the lines of old bricks. Mischievous frost or delinquent rain.

It became a game for Natalia. As she read, she would search for passages that her mother would appreciate. She would point out the line and inevitably her mother would kiss the top of her head approvingly.

~

One day in the library, when mother and daughter were slumped against the crook of the window, they heard a voice calling from outside.

Natalia turned to see a woman standing at the entrance to the hedge maze. She was dressed in a dark evening gown—one of mourning. Her hair cascaded over her shoulders in long sweeping curls and her face was solemn.

The woman said nothing more—merely stared for a long moment, dress blowing in the wind.

Neither Natalia nor her mother moved. Twice, the young girl's lip quivered, about to ask who the woman was and what was the matter, but breath caught in her throat. It felt as if the neck of her dress had grown tight—as if the blanket that covered her had grown oppressing and heavy. The blustering wind had died and even the sound of crashing waves grew distant.

Natalia heard nothing save for her own labored breathing and her mother's.

Then the woman turned and walked into the hedges. Disappeared into the maze.

Natalia gasped and felt hands clutching her, one around her head and the other around her shoulders. Her mother pulled Natalia close, the girl's head against her chest. Natalia felt her mother's chest heave and sob, and soon Natalia was crying too.

When their crying subsided, her mother grasped her face and stared at her—eyes shining brilliantly.

"I must find your father. Be still. Keep reading. Forget what you saw."

Then she left—running down the hall.

~

In a panic, Natalia followed—swept behind as if she was being pulled in her mother's wake.

The halls passed in a blur, paintings of dead Greensnows staring down indifferently at the child.

In the distance, she heard the desperate steps of her mother, and then the sudden quiet as those steps stopped in the hall of Father's study.

Natalia stopped at the corner of the hall—her mother was stopped just outside the door.

Then came the agitated steps of her father, the violent turning of the handle and creak as it swung open.

"Natalia, you musn't ru—" Her father's voice stopped short when he saw his wife standing there. His stoic face wavered for only a moment—like a crack of ice cutting across a frozen lake. "There, there, darling," he said. He pulled his wife close and ushered her into his study. Then shut the door.

Natalia slipped off her shoes and crept barefoot down the hall, the wood cold and unforgiving beneath her feet. She stopped just outside the door, straining to control her breathing.

"Are you sure it was her?" Father asked.

Her mother sobbed a reply.

"It doesn't make any sense," he said. "It doesn't make any damned sense. You're sure this is the first time you've seen her? What about Natalia, did she see? …Oh gods."

Finally came her mother's voice. "Is there anything in the library?"

"You know I don't keep those books there. Give me a moment."

There was a sliding of drawers and a shuffling of papers. Then came the soft leafing of pages.

"No. No," Father said. "It's much too soon—"

"It doesn't matter.I saw her." Her mother's voice was firm then, as if she'd found enough resolve for both of them. "Leave the books. I'll look through them myself. I—I can't hide from it any longer. I'm going to find Natalia."

Natalia was already off, shuffling as quickly as she could down the hall. She rounded the corner, picked up her shoes, and ran back toward the library.

She arrived there, breathless, and slipped her shoes back on. Then she stood, frozen—her gaze following the cliffs of books to the window. The two blankets lay in a heap on the floor, and Natalia couldn't bring herself to go to them or to the window. Not when the hedge maze lingered just outside, filled with some dreadful secret. A secret that terrified her mother so.

Her mother walked softly, stooped behind Natalia and wrapped her arms around her shoulders. "Do not be frightened," she said, "It cannot hurt you."

Though Natalia did not want to ask, the question tumbled unbidden from her mouth. "Who was that lady?"

Hands tugged her shoulders, and Natalia was turned to face her mother. Her eyes were red and glazed with tears, her lips hard-set.

"She wasn't real. It is a trick of the hedges."

Natalia shook her head in confusion.

"Do you remember what your father and I told you—to never go inside the maze?" The girl nodded. "It is to protect you. If you go into the maze you will never come back out."

"But what about Isiah and—"

Her mother winced and brought a hand to Natalia's mouth to silence her. "They are not Greensnows, and they are not women. Natalia, you must promise me that you will not go into the hedges. Swear it."

The young girl nodded and her mother stood, towering over her. "Let's go and see what Bernice is making for supper, and forget all about this day.

Natalia followed out of fear. She did not want to be left alone and did not want to think anymore on the events of that evening. She followed, but her mind wandered—as much as she tried to contain it.

Natalia wished she could forget that day and the face of the woman in the maze. The curly hair and face that reminded Natalia of her mother.

And so, Natalia's childhood passed, the young maid wandering the grounds and nestling beneath blankets reading—

The whole of it punctuated with nightmares of the hedge maze. Sometimes, Natalia was peering down through the window, watching the visage walk into the hedges. Sometimes, her mother was down there, disappearing into that green void. And other times, Natalia would look up at the manor, at the library window, and watch as her mother panicked and banged on the glass—before Natalia turned and walked into the hedges.

~

Years passed on Greensnow Estate, and Natalia grew into a young woman—a portrait of her mother.

Meanwhile, the more the world changed around Natalia, the more she struggled to stay the same. She kept her morning walks of the estate, and her seclusion in the library.

But as she grew of age, her parents dragged her further and further into adulthood. Her parents took turns teaching her about the estate—about how to manage it and keep records of purchases and investments. She also learned about the other houses of the Frozen Isles; which ones were desirable partners, both in trade and in relations.

At that same time, her mother strove to teach her the ways of a desirable young woman, for the expectation was that she would marry in the coming years. There was, after all, the preservation of the Greensnow Estate to consider—this became a weekly reminder as Natalia neared twenty.

All the while, she had recurring nightmares of the hedge maze. She stayed silent about these, not wanting to trouble her mother or father.

Mother, of which, seemed not to have the time for such concerns. She buried herself in work, and came to the library less. The playfulness was gone from her face, and sometimes Natalia felt as if mother were a different woman altogether.

More like the woman from the hedges.

It was in her nineteenth year—much later than she would care to admit—that Natalia realized why the ominous figure looked so familiar.

She was walking down the hall near her father's study; the hall filled with dozens of Greensnow family portraits.

Natalia almost fainted when she saw the portrait of her grandmother. Grandma was even wearing the same dark evening dress, hair cascading the same way over her shoulders. Her face looked wrinkled in disapproval, the same as if she'd walked out of a nightmare.

It was two days after that Natalia finally worked up the courage to ask about her grandma.

Natalia found her mother at the cliffs that morning. She stared out over the frozen sea, lost in thought. Her curls billowed in the wind.

Natalia walked up and stood beside her mother. The wind was biting.

"Why did grandma go into the hedge maze?"

Mother didn't answer—not for some time.

"Because she had to."

Natalia shook her head. "But you said—"

"She had to. There are things you don't understand, Natalia. This is one of them."

"I'm not a child anymore."

"Yes, you are. You don't need to know yet."

Natalia felt as if she'd been slapped. She'd been rebuked similarly over the years, but never so casually—never about something so important.

"Why did we see her that day?"

"I don't know why her visage appeared that day." Mother's gaze fell to the cliffs. "It is an omen, Natalia. One that shouldn't have come yet."

Again, her mother fell silent. Then she turned to her daughter, her eyes glassy, her face red and numb with the cold. "Because those that are gone are not gone completely." Her lips quivered. "There are things about the world—things about our family, my child, that can't be explained or reasoned with. They cannot be bought or bartered.

"Swear again that you will not go into the hedges."

"Did grandma go into the hedges?"

Mother paused. "Yes."

"But she came back out that day."

"Her *visage* did. That thing was not your grandmother."

"But you said she was not gone, not completely."

Mother shook her head in frustration. "It doesn't matter. Swear to me, child."

"I'm just trying to—"

"Swear it!"

Natalia jumped at the outburst, then nodded meekly.

"Say it aloud."

"I swear."

Mother nodded and turned back to the sea. "Good. Now go back inside, child, before you catch your death out here."

Natalia turned to go, but asked, "What about you?"

"I'll be right behind you."

Natalia walked back to the manor, turning several times to see if her mother was, in fact, right behind her. She wasn't. Her Mother stayed at the cliffs until the sun was nearly set.

Mother spent the rest of the evening by the fire, huddled under blankets.

Natalia spent the rest of the evening peeking in on her, but she never moved from the chair.

~

Several times after that, Natalia would ask about the hedge maze or about her grandmother, but her parents refused to answer, or outright rebuked her. Eventually, they pretended not to hear. It was as if the whole ordeal had never happened.

Natalia stopped asking. She wasn't sure when she stopped, only that she noticed her parents growing steadily happier again—her mother grew steadily happier. The melancholy that had plagued her seemed gone completely, as if a fog had lifted.

And so Natalia chose to forget.

She let herself get swept away in books and traveling with her parents to other estates. She was at *the prime age to marry.* Those words became her mother's mantra when they were together. She met half a dozen suitors from those families— young men with dreams and ambitions that seemed almost comical to Natalia. They were in the Frozen Isles, after all. How much ambition could one have at the bottom of the world?

There was one young man, though, that captivated her. His name was Willem. Heir to the Danzborough estate. His family did business all over the world, and he quickly took to telling tales of the mainlands of Eadruin and Ozequn. He wrote letters to her while he was away, telling of warm ports, clear water, and balmy locales.

It warmed her to hear such places, awakening longings in her that she had only felt shades of in years past.

While there were men pining after her that were content with their place in the Frozen Isles, here was a man who wanted the world *and* who wanted her.

~

So it went for three years. Natalia and Willem exchanging letters and summering on the Danzborough estate under the watchful eye of her father.

The courting was as much for her father as it was for Natalia. Should something have happened to him, the estate would pass to Natalia's uncle, Hernando. But should Natalia and Willem wed, the estate would pass to Natalia and then to her children. As such, her father was keen to keep an eye on his investments.

Those trips were the most she had ever spoken to her father. Always about business.

Sometimes in their quieter moments, usually traversing the Gelid Sea and huddled with candles below decks, she worked up the nerve to ask him about something other than that—sometimes he even humored her.

Once, she asked him how he and mother met. He had summered in the Isles that year and heard talk of mother. That she was fond of reading and loathed travel as much as he did. That was what bonded them—not something romantic like Natalia had read in so many books over the years… Just that they didn't like to travel.

Up until that point, Natalia had been aghast at the banality of it. But then her father grew conspiratorially quiet as he continued. He said that *it wasn't that he wanted to see the world. The world was so very big and lonely. He just wanted someone that would share some small corner of it with him.*

Natalia thought of WIllem. She imagined him striding from the deck of a merchant ship and onto a faraway dock, and imagined herself beside him. In that moment, she wasn't sure where life would take her, but she was certain that she wanted to go with Willem.

~

Natalia Greensnow and Willem Danzborough courted for those three years.

Natalia had never known such happiness or such wonder. She read about places all over the world, read about impossible places, intriguing mystery and deep romance—

Yet it all paled in comparison to the real thing.

~

That summer, Willem visited the Greensnow estate for two weeks. Natalia nearly knocked him over when she ran into his arms on the docks.

In the mornings, they toured the grounds. She showed him all her family's markers and all her precious hideaways. They took breakfast in seclusion and often forgot about it—lost in each other's warmth and passion. In the afternoons, Willem and her father attended to business. Every evening, Willem came back to her, and the two would read in the library or talk by the fire.

So it went, the lovers circling each other in their own small orbit, their own small corner of the world.

It was almost perfect, but such things never last.

~

"What about that?" Willem asked, pointing out the library window at the hedge maze. He smiled wryly. "I don't think you've taken me there yet."

He was right. Natalia had made a point to take him everywhere else on the island and to avoid the hedge maze out back. She'd even tried to keep his attention away from that particular window in the library.

But that day, she'd spent too long looking for a book and her lover's attention had wandered.

So Natalia thought quickly, and said, "There's maintenance that needs to be done, I'm afraid. Father's declared it off limits."

Willem smiled. "When has that stopped us?"

Natalia shook her head. "This time it will."

"Come now, Natalia…" He stared and must have seen the hesitation written on her face. "Say no more. I've left other mysteries fallow. What's one more?"

~

Two different mornings near the end of his visit, Natalia and Willem walked hand in hand out of the manor to find her mother standing at the cliff's edge and looking out over the Gelid Sea.

Willem turned to walk to her, but Natalia stood firm.

"Shouldn't we say good morning?" he asked.

Natalia shook her head, remembering how troubled her mother had been the last time she was standing in such a spot.

"We shouldn't trouble her," she replied.

The next morning, they found her mother standing in the same spot. Again, Willem stopped and stared across the grounds.

"Are you sure she's alright?" Willem asked.

"She's just melancholy, I think. She'll be fine in the 'morrow."

~

It was the day before Willem was due to leave. They walked the grounds as they had every other day, but that morning they stopped before they entered the manor and went to the cliffs overlooking the Gelid Sea.

At first, when Willem was leading her away from the manor, she worried that they would find her mother again in that lonely spot. But she wasn't there that morning.

Natalia and Willem were alone. They stood, hand in hand, staring out at the icy sea. The clouds swirled that day, filling the sky. It felt as if they were standing in the middle of the world.

Willem turned, stooped to one knee, and proposed to her.

Natalia accepted, breathlessly, and the two embraced on the cliff side, forgetting everything else.

When their passionate kisses smoldered, Natalia and Willem returned to the manor, seeking both her father and her mother to tell them of the news.

Natalia assumed that her mother would be in the library, but when the lovers entered, they didn't find any trace of her—save for a blanket unfurled on the floor by the back window.

"Perhaps she's in her room," Willem said.

But Natalia was already walking toward the blanket—toward the window. Heart in her throat. Afraid to breathe. She felt deathly cold as she peered through the glass and down to the hedge maze.

Her mother was standing there at the entrance of the hedges, staring up at Natalia. She wore her dark dress and evening cloak, wearing an expression of stillborn calm.

Natalia's face wrinkled in a silent plea, but her mother was already turning. Already walking into the maze.

Natalia wasn't sure when she started screaming—she only knew that suddenly Willem was upon her, her father a breath later.

Her father needed only to look down through the window to know what had happened. In a panic, he told Willem to stay with his daughter.

Natalia fell to the floor, and Willem fell with her. They sat together intertwined, his arms wrapped around her, Natalia's head buried in his shoulder. Her chest heaving in painful sobs.

~

The men searched the hedge maze. By the time Natalia's father and the workers emerged, the sun had nearly set. It sat on the horizon, bloated and bleeding.

Natalia ran down from the library to the hedge maze, Willem right behind her.

"She's gone," her father said. His eyes were glassy and sullen.

Fear gave way to rage and Natalia pushed toward the hedges, but her father and Willem grasped her arms and held her back.

Natalia screamed and gasped for breath, and finally, when the fight had left her body, she stopped struggling.

"Where is she?" Natalia asked, eyes burning in the cold wind.

"She's gone," her father whispered.

"Gone like grandma?"

Her father glanced up at her, sudden fear gripping him. He turned to Willem and the workers. "Leave us."

Out of the corner of her eye, Willem looked to her, but Natalia didn't meet his eyes. Willem walked off with the others.

In spite of the burning in her chest, Natalia's voice was forceful, like she were dredging up hot coals with each mouthful of steam.

"Tell me what happened to her or so help me I'll go in after her."

Her father breathed deep. "It's our curse. The Greensnows found this estate some generations ago."

"I know that. I *already* know that—"

"Not founded, dear. They *found* this place."

"I don't understand."

"This place was already here, immaculate, and abandoned." His voice was measured as he spoke, as if he had rehearsed the words before, but never spoken them to another. "Your mother's family settled the island, brought their own workers.

They made it their own. For some years, it was a mystery what happened to the previous family. We found their family ledgers, saw the premature deaths, but they were all written as natural happenings.

"Your great-great grandmother discovered the truth about the hedge maze. It is a soul well of sorts. Those that go into it never come back out."

Natalia shook her head. "But you and—"

"It only takes the women of the family. Every so many years, it calls to the woman of the house."

Natalia unconsciously took a step back from her father. "Why didn't you tell me? Why didn't mother tell me?"

His face twisted in pain. "Why would we hang such a cloud over your head? Others have tried to break whatever magic lies in the hedges, but no amount of mages, diviners, or theologians had any effect. Some magic is too old to be reckoned with. Too powerful to be denied." He gestured to the sea past the cliffs. "It's like trying to deny the waves."

A sickening feeling twisted in Natalia's stomach at the thought of so much pain—such a curse—right there on the grounds—just beyond her father.

"Why didn't you do—"

"Don't you dare!" he seethed. "What would you have me do? What could I possibly do?"

"You could have left!"

Her father shook his head. "She couldn't leave. The hedges wouldn't let her."

"I don't understand." When her father didn't respond, Natalia said, "Willem asked me to marry him."

Her father's face contorted, a twisted mixture of pain and happiness. "Oh my child. That's wonderful. I'll make arrangements for his things to be brought over—"

Natalia was aghast. "We're not staying here. Not after this! I'm leaving with Willem, as soon as I can."

"No! No!" Her father grabbed her arms, his face crazed. "You mustn't. He must come here. You don't understand. The hedges won't let you leave!"

Natalia pushed her father away. "You expect me to stay here and wait to die?"

Her father just turned with his hands clasped around his head, muttering, "You don't understand. You don't understand."

Natalia turned and ran for the manor, leaving her father in front of the hedge maze and alone with his ramblings.

~

Natalia ran to the library, and began searching the shelves for any books about the Frozen Isles or about curses or about her family's estate.

Willem found her when she was only a quarter way through the shelves. He waited behind her meekly, without saying a word.

She turned back to him three times, before she finally broke down and fell into his arms. She held him close, choking down her distress.

He didn't have to ask—Natalia told him everything that her father had. Even told him about seeing her grandmother's visage when she was younger.

Willem held her close and listened intently.

And when she was done, she looked up at him, a swirl of emotions inside her. What would he say? Would he turn and leave? Would he leave her in this desolate, cursed place, never to return? Would he even say goodbye, or would he silently walk out of her life?

"You can't stay here," he finally said. "I've seen my share of curses and strange *things*. You can't stay here. I won't let you. I won't leave you here."

Natalia had been holding her breath in anticipation, and the sudden release of tension made her knees nearly buckle, like the crashing of a wave.

"What will we do?" she asked.

Willem glanced around the room and back to her several times. "My house has mages that might be able to help. I will send for them. I can send for others." His eyes fell to Natalia's. "I will need to leave, but I will be back as soon as I can. I'll turn right 'round and come back with enough to tear you free of this place."

Natalia's eyes were watering. She believed him, she did.

They went to bed that night, taking comfort in each other. That they were the only force in the world that decided their fates. Natalia fell into a dreamless, peaceful sleep.

~

The next morning, the merchant ship *Little Sparrow* came for Willem, and Natalia saw him off at the dock.

It was cloudy that morning. The sky was a swirling sea of grays and greens, blotting out the morning sun.

"Two weeks," Willem said as he held her close. "Not even a letter could reach you as quick. I'll come for you, I will."

She believed him, with all her heart.

Natalia and Willem pulled each other close and kissed goodbye. She felt a swirl of weakness as she melted in his arms, and a kindling of hope.

Since meeting Willem, she'd known what so many story-books had talked about—those indescribable feelings that had seemed so foreign, like trying to explain the taste of a spice from a forgotten corner of the world.

Natalia had stood on that same harbor before, kissing Willem goodbye, watching him sail away. She'd felt the sun on her shoulders and the salt spray on her lips. But that day, it felt as if she was standing there for the first time, feeling more alive than she ever had.

Natalia wept again, this time tears of hope and joy as her betrothed faded over the horizon.

And when his ship was gone, she turned and walked across the dock and the grounds, back to the manor—all the while kindled by the hope inside her.

~

It wasn't until she walked into the manor and felt the oppressive silence that the day's events weighed on her. She stood in the entry hall staring up at the grand staircase for so long. Alone, save for the silence.

Sometime later, her father appeared at the top of the stairs, glass of brown liquor in hand. His eyes were glassy in the fading light. He stopped and leaned on the railing.

"You've damned him," he said. "You've damned that poor boy."

Silence gave way to smoldering anger.

"Like you damned me," Natalia replied.

Though her lips twitched with repugnance and insults, Natalia said none of them. Somehow, silence was more fitting. Her parents had neglected to tell her of their family's curse. Neglected to warn her. They had chosen silence instead.

So Natalia turned silence against her father. Held it up like some terrible mirror. She would let the quiet say all the things that she could not.

She left him standing on the stairs. Natalia went to her room and slept.

~

Two weeks passed, just as Willem said it would. She spent the days wandering the grounds and reading, just as she always had. While Natalia Greensnow lived on the island, her mind was everywhere else—anywhere else. Most of the time, her thoughts were with Willem.

Natalia didn't speak a word to her father. Twice, he came into the library. One of those times, speaking quietly to her from afar—though Natalia didn't listen and didn't reply.

She pretended that her father didn't exist.

~

Two weeks to the day that Willem left, Isiah came to the library.

The boy worker that she had known had grown along with her. He'd grown tall and strong, and was just as meek as ever.

Isiah walked into the library, clutching a letter. He set it on the table in front of her and walked away.

It bore the Danzborough family seal and was addressed to her, but as Natalia turned to open it, she realized that it wasn't written by Willem.

Natalia tore the end of it open so desperately that she tore a sliver off the top of the corner of the fold. She opened the marred letter and read it, breath caught in her throat.

Natalia Greensnow,

It is with deepest sadness and regret that we write to you with this news. The merchant vessel Little Sparrow *was lost in a squall in transit from the Greensnow estate to Danzborough estate. All souls on board were lost, including our Willem...*

It felt as if the world had dropped out from beneath Natalia. She felt weak and nauseous. The letter dropped from her hand before she could finish it. Violent sobs wracked her chest, and she covered her mouth in feeble attempt to quiet herself.

Day faded into night. Natalia didn't rise from the floor. Waves of sadness overtook her periodically, giving way to numbness before inevitably ebbing back to grief. She felt as if she'd been hurled over the edge of the cliffs and was drowning in the icy waves of the sea.

No one came for her that night, or if they did, they came as quietly as specters and turned back before Natalia saw them.

It was deep into the night before Natalia uttered the most dreadful part of all—

No one was coming for her.

Willem wasn't coming for her.

It was in that dreadful moment that Natalia heard the faint voice of her mother calling from beyond the library window.

~

Natalia Greensnow woke early the next morning on the floor of the library. She'd spent the night drifting in and out of fitful sleep, and fending off dreams that defied memory.

She wrapped a blanket around her and pulled it taut around her shoulders, then walked out of empty Greensnow manor.

She walked around the side of the building, frozen dew crunching beneath her feet, around to the hedge maze.

Her mother stood at the entrance, clad in her favorite purple. She smiled warmly, hands clasped in front of her expectantly.

The wind grew still as Natalia approached the hedge maze, and she felt a chill run down her neck. Her heart was thumping in her chest so powerfully that Natalia felt it might leap out and run of its own accord.

"Hello, Natalia. It's so good to see you."

Natalia stared at her mother in disbelief. "How—how do I know that you're really her?"

Her mother just shook her head, as if the question were the most childish thing her daughter could've said.

"It's me," was all she replied.

Natalia looked over her mother's form, searching for any sign of blemish or imperfection—anything so Natalia could conclude that it was a fraud. Anything that would let her believe that this apparition wasn't her mother.

But Natalia knew it wasn't true. Somehow, her mother stood before her. Through some dark magic or curse…

"How?" Natalia asked, the word falling from her lips.

Her mother smiled. "This island—our home—is special. A long time ago, something happened here. A promise was made, power was bartered or a curse was struck… Something fallowed the ground. Made it ripe for us. When the Greensnows settled this island, we were rewarded with bountiful lives and trade."

"But what was the cost, mother? There's always a cost."

Mother frowned. "The cost isn't as great as you think. Every so many years, a lady Greensnow gives herself to the hedge maze."

"I don't understand—"

Behind her mother, the hedges began to change, or perhaps they had been changing. In the tiny curling branches, and in the dark spaces between the leaves, thousands of tiny eyes stared back at Natalia. They twisted toward her and blinked like sea foam.

Natalia stared, frozen in shock.

"You don't understand," her mother said. "I am still here, Natalia. I never left you. I might live in the hedges, but I'm still here. You could come talk to me every day if you like."

"Where is grandma?"

Her mother stood there, mouth half open as if she didn't know what to say. Finally, she said, "She's here too. But… For now you can only talk to me." Behind her, eyes boiled in the hedges.

Natalia's gaze fell to her mother's feet, and then she looked across the fields—she couldn't bear to look at the hedges. Then she turned to walk off—

"Where are you going?" Mother asked.

"I… I need some time to think."

"There's nothing to think about, child."

Natalia nodded curtly and walked off across the field. Her whole body was tense as she walked, ready if she needed to break out into a run. Twice, she turned back to see if her mother or something worse was following her—

But her mother was gone, and the hedges were back to their harmless, immobile green.

Natalia walked all the way to the cliffs overlooking the Gelid Sea. Tears streamed down her face and turned to frost in the wind.

Emotion became a storm within her. No matter what good had come from this place, none could assuage the thought of her mother's entrapment, Willem's death, or the dark fate that awaited Natalia.

She looked out over the sea, the churning icy and foam, and knew she had only one recourse.

Her last thought was peace, the ebb of the waves, and the stillness that she would find at the bottom.

Natalia Greensnow leapt from the cliffs. The wind grew to a roar and her heart beat in her throat.

She was halfway down when something seized her violently—roots and vines stretched out from cliffs, grasping her limbs and halting her fall. For a moment, she was held aloft and completely unable to move.

Natalia didn't scream until she felt the vines tugging and lurching—dragging her back up the cliffs.

~

There was no escape for Natalia—for the forgotten magic of the hedge maze kept her from harm and kept away all those that would aid her in leaving. Once she stowed away aboard a ship. Two days in it was capsized. A day later, Natalia washed up on the beach of the island. Other attempts to take her own life were similarly rebuked.

No matter how much she begged and pleaded and prayed, no help came for her.

Years passed on the estate. Eventually, horror faded to memory, ground away like rocks beneath the waves. Reduced to sand.

Natalia loved again. The family of Greensnow grew. Her children grew.

They walked the grounds with her and explored uncountable words in the pages of the library, just as Natalia had with her mother before.

And one day, when her daughters were ten and fourteen, Natalia heard the call of her mother again.

She heeded it, walking out of the manor without a word and leaving her children and husband behind.

Only her father saw. He stood on the stairwell, his skin pickled by drink and despair. He watched and said nothing.

Natalia walked to the hedge maze, to her mother's voice calling from deep within it. Her call became a plea, became a scream. She was fading, her voice growing faint, weak.

Natalia stopped at the threshold of the hedges and found the thousands of eyes waiting for her, boiling like sea foam in the leaves.

Dread and calm swirled within her—dread of the unknown fate that lay just a few short steps away, some unknowable, unholy end. And calm, for she knew that she had no choice.

Natalia turned to look upon the manor one last time. Her gaze rose up the walls, and found the library window.

And found her youngest daughter staring back—her face contorted in a silent scream.

END

Thank you for Reading

I hope you enjoyed reading these stories as much as I enjoyed writing them. If you did, I would greatly appreciate a short review on Amazon or your favorite book website. Reviews are crucial for any author, and even just a line or two can make a huge difference.

On writing

Vulgar Display of Power

Oh, Sircius Everdeath. You're one of my favorites. There's just something about writing the bad guy. Heroes have so many *rules*. Bad guys, not so much.

I'm not sure what else there is to say about this one, other than Sircius continuing his evil campaign across the continent of Ozequn. I've got a couple more stories planned for our favorite lich. I'm excited to see where exactly his campaign goes and where he winds up among the other short stories I have planned.

To Walk in Dreams

Dreams are a touchy subject in fiction. To me, they're one of the best examples of a prominent plot device that is used too often and rarely used well.

Sometimes, I wonder why I do these things to myself.

Dreams aside, one of the most amazing things about writing interconnected stories like this is building an actual world. The more stories I write, the more *alive* this world feels. Maybe there are parts of *Tales from Another World* that would've lent themselves better to a novel format, but I still stand by these interconnected short stories, and I feel like they've given me a hell of a sandbox to play in.

The creepy *thing* from Tylor's dream has a much larger part to play in the *TFAW*. It makes a quick cameo in *A Battleaxe and a Metal Arm 15*. If you've been following the story, you can guess which of the main characters might come to blows with it down the road.

The creature's name is *Nimicus*.

The Lightning Nymph

Of all the stories in this volume, I think *The Lightning Nymph* is my favorite. I'm not sure if that's a blasphemous thing for a writer to admit or not, but there it is. No take-backsies.

When I get an idea for a story, most of the time they come half-formed, or with only a single scene or character at first. *The Lightning Nymph* struck me the same way lightning hit Len at the end of this story. I knew everything, all of the scenes, and exactly how it would end. And I knew I had to write it down as quickly as I could.

The Lightning Nymph is about obsession, and the often dangerous and debilitating lengths that some of us will go to in pursuit of it.

Hanging Lanterns

I first started writing Hanging Lanterns with the intention of making it an audio first publication. I wound up including it in this volume, but I think the story retained most of the feel of spoken-word.

It's hard to write about the history of a fictional world. Usually it has to be sprinkled in throughout a longer work. Info dumping is what it's called when a writer shoves in pages of exposition about the world. It's possible to do an info dump well, but it's difficult because they usually bring the story to a screeching halt. Hopefully I've done alright with this one by incorporating it into another story.

Guardians of the Forest

I'm not sure if it's true of all genres of stories, but fantasy stories start in the midst of change. Sometimes the kingdom is in upheaval or ancient magic is brought back to the world. It's one of my favorite tropes, and for this story, I wanted to allude to that long lost magic. The Resnocti used to be guardians of the forest, but they're gone—swallowed up by something. If you're reading *A Battleaxe and a Metal Arm*, then you might recognize the giant owls.

In *Tales from Another World*, forests are places of shadow and magic, or at least, they used to be.

The Hedge Maze of Greensnow Manor

I feel like I've had the idea for this story rattling around for a while. I was hesitant to include it in *Tales from Another World*, since it is quite long when compared to stories in previous volumes, but I think it got pared down enough. I have a soft spot for old Victorian manors and castles, and all the spooky secrets buried within their walls. *THMGM* is an ode to the gothic horror stories set there.

Curses are another recurring theme in these volumes, and this is reminiscent of the curse that plagued Clayman Brook and the family that worked the narrow stretch of water. Though Lop may not look much like Natalia, they are both bound by a family curse that they cannot escape.

Connect with the Author

If you want to stay up to date on the latest about Samuel's publishing news and blog, check out his website and consider signing up for his monthly newsletter.

www.SamuelFlemingBooks.com

Samuel can also be found on Tiktok, Facebook, and Reddit.

Samuel Fleming is a Science Fiction and Fantasy author.

He grew up in Maryland, spending most of his time swimming and writing. Swimming gave him a lot of time to daydream, so the two hobbies complemented each other well. Idle day dreams turned into stories, some of which stuck with him for years. These days he swims a little less and writes a lot more.

He loves a good story no matter the medium: Books, TV, video games, comics, tabletop RPG's, or podcasts–most of which he attempts to share with his wife and three kids, and occasionally on his blog.

www.ingramcontent.com/pod-product-compliance
Lightning Source LLC
Chambersburg PA
CBHW030651190726
48286CB00008B/2760